Henry Morford

Celebration at Tammany Hall

on Friday, July 4th, 1862

Henry Morford

Celebration at Tammany Hall
on Friday, July 4th, 1862

ISBN/EAN: 9783741124969

Manufactured in Europe, USA, Canada, Australia, Japa

Cover: Foto ©Andreas Hilbeck / pixelio.de

Manufactured and distributed by brebook publishing software
(www.brebook.com)

Henry Morford

Celebration at Tammany Hall

SOCIETY OF TAMMANY;

COLUMBIAN ORDER.

———◆———

CELEBRATION

AT

TAMMANY HALL,

On FRIDAY, JULY 4th, 1862.

INCLUDING

THE POEM,

By HENRY MORFORD, Esq.;

THE ORATION,

By Hon. CHARLES P. DALY.

PUBLISHED BY ORDER OF THE SOCIETY.

NEW YORK:

BAPTIST & TAYLOR, STEAM BOOK AND JOB PRINTERS,
SUN BUILDING, COR. FULTON AND NASSAU STS.

1862.

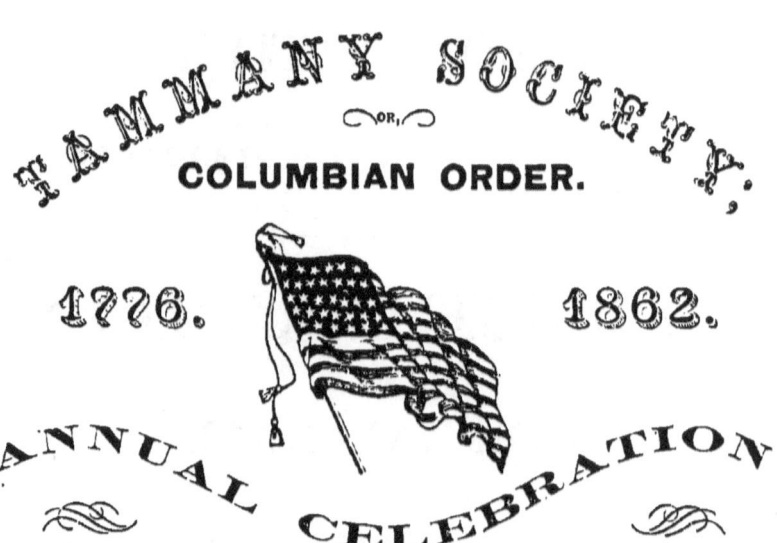

TAMMANY SOCIETY,

—OR,—

COLUMBIAN ORDER.

1776. 1862.

ANNUAL CELEBRATION

IN HONOR OF THE EIGHTY-SIXTH ANNIVERSARY

—OF—

American Independence,

AT TAMMANY HALL,

—◦✕◦—

On FRIDAY, JULY 4th, 1862.

— ◀●▶ —

New York:

BAPTIST & TAYLOR, STEAM BOOK AND JOB PRINTERS, SUN BUILDINGS,

COR. FULTON AND NASSAU STREETS.

1862.

CELEBRATION

BY THE

TAMMANY SOCIETY;

OR,

COLUMBIAN ORDER,

OF THE

86th Anniversary of American Independence,

AT

TAMMANY HALL,

FRIDAY, JULY 4th, 1862.

------◄•►------

In accordance with their unvarying custom since 1789, the members of the Tammany Society met in the "Grand Council Chamber" of the "Old Wigwam," on the Fourth of July, to celebrate, with appropriate ceremonies and in the manner prescribed by their Constitution, the Birth-day of the Nation. At a Preliminary Meeting of the Members, the general charge of the festivities had been intrusted to a

Special Committee,

Consisting of—

  Sachem DANIEL E. DELAVAN, *Chairman,*

    " DOUGLAS TAYLOR,

    " JAMES B. NICHOLSON,

who, having made the necessary arrangements, issued the following Programme for the day:

SOCIETY OF TAMMANY; OR, COLUMBIAN ORDER.

CELEBRATION OF THE EIGHTY-SIXTH ANNIVERSARY OF OUR NATIONAL INDEPENDENCE.

The members of the TAMMANY SOCIETY will meet at the Old Wigwam, at half-past eleven o'clock, A. M., on FRIDAY, JULY 4, 1862; at twelve o'clock the doors of the Grand Council Chamber will be thrown open ; the Sachems, Warriors and Chiefs will assemble on the platform in the large hall.

The CECILIAN BRASS BAND will perform national airs until the commencement of the exercises, which will be at ONE O'CLOCK, P. M., PRECISELY.

ORDER OF EXERCISES.

OVERTURE—National Airs............................Cecilian Brass Band.

OPENING ADDRESS,...............................Grand Sachem WATERBURY.

NATIONAL HYMN—"*My Country, 'Tis of Thee,*" will then be sung by Professor COLBURN and TWENTY-FOUR Boys, accompanied on the Piano by a celebrated musical artist.

THE DECLARATION OF INDEPENDENCE will be read by Bro. GEORGE W. McLEAN.

CHORUS—"*Red, White and Blue,*" — Prof. COLBURN and Twenty-four Boys, with Piano accompaniment.

Brother HOSEA B. PERKINS will recite ELIZA COOK'S ODE TO WASHINGTON.

SONG AND CHORUS—"*The Drum Tap Rattles Through the Land,*" sung by Prof. COLBURN and Pupils, with Piano accompaniment.

After which HENRY MORFORD, Esq. will read his patriotic POEM, composed for the occasion, entitled "TAMMANY AND THE UNION."

CHORUS—Patriotic Hymn—"*Forever,*" sung by Prof. COLBURN and Twenty-four Boys, Piano accompaniment.

ORATION..Hon. CHARLES P. DALY.

The exercises will conclude with the "*Star Spangled Banner,*" sung by Prof. COLBURN and boys, accompanied by the Cecilian Brass Band, the audience rising and joining in the chorus.

After which the Banquet Room will be thrown open, where the "Waters of the Great Spring" will flow plenteously, and where distinguished brethren will respond to appropriate sentiments, and patriotic songs will be given by an efficient Glee Club.

COMMITTEE OF ARRANGEMENTS.

Sachem John A. Dix,
Sachem Elijah F. Purdy,
Sachem Richard B. Connolly,
Sachem Peter B. Sweeny,
Treasurer George E. Baldwin,
Sagamore G. S. Messerve,

RICHARD WINNE, *Scribe.*

Sachem John Kelly,
Sachem Isaac Bell,
Sachem Jas. B. Nicholson,
Sachem Daniel E. Delavan,

Sachem Thomas Dunlap,
Sachem Edward Cooper,
Sachem John E. Develin,
Sachem Douglas Taylor,
Secretary C. C. Childs,
Wiskinkie S. C. Duryea.

HENRY VANDEWATER, *Father of the Council.*

COMMITTEE OF MEMBERS OF THE SOCIETY.

Daniel F. Tiemann,
Emanuel B. Hart,
John R. Brady,
Andrew V. Stout,
M. T. Brennan,
Smith Ely, Jr.
Anthony L. Robertson,
James Murphy,
James Lynch,
Geo. W. McLean,
C. Godfrey Gunther,
Andre Froment,
L. F. Harrison,
Andrew H. Green,
Thos. B. Tappan,
George G. Barnard,
Jno. Y. Savage, Jr.,

Chas. J. Chipp,
John T. Hoffman,
John M. Barbour,
Thos. C. Fields,
William Miner,
Albert Cardoza,
Henry Hilton,
Michael Connolly,
Aaron B. Rollins,
John R. Briggs,
Wilson G. Hunt,
Wm. McMurray,
Fredk. D. Vulte,
William P. Powers,
Ralph Bogart,
Wm. C. Conner,
John Richardson,

Augustus Schell,
Henry L. Clinton,
William M. Tweed,
John T. Henry,
John S. Giles,
Samuel J. Tilden,
Jesiah W. Brown,
Wm. H. Leonard,
Wm. J. Peck,
Thomas Byrnes,
David A. Fowler,
John H. McCunn,
Thomas W. Adams,
Anson Herrick,
John Clancy,
Thos. K. Downing,
Malcolm Campbell,

Nathaniel Jarvis, Jr.
George H. E. Lynch,
Edward Sanford,
Robert C. McIntire,
William B. Clerke,
Harvey F. Aubery,
Moses D. Gale,
John Fitch,
Edmund L. Hearne,
John Eagan,
A. T. Gallagher,
Peter Moneghan,
Wm. Murphy,
Jefferson Brown,
George Smith,
Walter Roche,
Joseph D. Baldwin.

CASPER C. CHILDS, *Secretary.*

NELSON J. WATERBURY, *Grand Sachem.*

In response to this call, the members of the Society and their friends, to the number of two thousand, assembled in the "Grand Council Chamber" which was superbly decorated with the flags of all nations. A splendid transparency of General JACKSON was draped in the national colors; on the sides of the room were conspicuously displayed the banners of the Society, and the insignia of the thirteen original States; and the portraits of WASHINGTON, LAFAYETTE, JEFFERSON, POLK, CLAY, and WEBSTER, occupied prominent positions on the walls of the old Wigwam.

The Sachems and Officers of the Society, with their distinguished guests, having taken their places on the platform, the band performed a selection of national airs, after which the large assemblage was called to order by the Grand Sachem, who made the following introductory remarks:

ADDRESS

OF

HON. NELSON J. WATERBURY.

BROTHERS AND FRIENDS:—In accordance with immemorial usage and with the constitution of the Tammany Society, the doors of the great Wigwam are this day thrown open to all the friends of liberty who may desire to participate with us in the celebration of the anniversary of our National Independence. [cheers] The Tammany Society and the Society of the Cincinnati each took root in the pure soil of the revolutionary era, and they are the only organizations formed at that early period which have remained until the present time. Each has regularly commemorated the return of this sacred day. The Tammany Society is devoted now, as it was at the period of its formation, to our national Constitution, and to those principles of civil liberty upon which our government is founded, and upon which alone it can be perpetuated; [cheers] and I take great pleasure in saying that it has grown with the growth of our nation, and that it has ever been the hallowed spot where all the friends of our country could gather, and where people from other parts of the world could devote themselves to freedom, under the protection of those sacred principles. [*loud cheers.*]

My friends, there never was a time when it was more incumbent upon every man who loves liberty—who values the freedom of his country, to celebrate the birthday of our independence; there never was a time, I say, in our history when it was more incumbent upon us to do so, than it is now. [*cheers*] We are at a crisis when a wicked rebellion has raised its foul head to overthrow and destroy the best government that the world has ever known; and we are here to day surrounded by other circumstances which make the present a peculiarly trying time. This is the second Fourth of July since this war commenced. When we assembled here one year ago there was no voice throughout the northern States which pretended to be loyal to the Constitution of our country, which did not also profess to be willing to uphold and maintain that Constitution in all its sacredness and in all its parts. [*loud cheers*] That was the doctrine which was universally proclaimed only one year ago; and the Congress of the United States, by a vote nearly unanimous, passed a resolution pledging itself that the war should not be waged to overthrow or interfere with the rights or established institutions of the States of this Union. [*cheers*] Only one year has rolled around, and during a large portion of that year, very many of the men who voted for that resolution have been striving, basely striving, even with the crime of perjury upon their souls to destroy what they pledged themselves to sustain. [*groans*] We find even in our own section of the country, among men who professed to be willing to sustain this government, and to uphold it against all the dangers which

may threaten it, we find men who are more dangerous to its
perpetuity—to the success of the holiest of causes, or as dangerous at least, as the traitors who are in arms against us at the
South. [*hear, hear and cheers*] By the machinations of these
men the gallant young general who has been sent forward to
fight the battles of his country [*enthusiastic cheers for McClellan*]
• under more trying circumstances than ever before surrounded
any man, has been compelled with his gallant soldiers to face,
upon the deadly battle field, three times their own number.

Most unfortunate, or if not unfortunate, at least mortifying to
us Democrats, is the fact, that this disaster—the situation in
which that General and his army are placed, and all the consequences which may arise from it, are the work of a man who
one year ago pretended to be a Democrat: a man who was
selected by President Lincoln and placed in the War Department because he was a Democrat, and, I doubt not, as a grace-
ful recognition by the President, of the generous support he had
received from the northern democracy in the struggle to maintain our country. We have found, however, as we will always
find, that the worst of all men is a renegade. We need not be
surprised, therefore, that when Edwin M. Stanton took office,
and betrayed the party to which he had hitherto professed to
belong, that from that time forward he has been the fitting tool
of the Abolitionists, [*groans*] and has been their instrument—
their mean instrument to accomplish their damnable and detest-
able purposes [*groans.*]

A VOICE—Down with the Abolitionists.

Mr. WATERBURY—But, my friends, our cause is not to be lost
by the treachery or misconduct of any man or any set of men.
[*cheers.*] This Government: the Constitution of our country:
the Union of these States are to be maintained under all circumstances, come what may. [*enthusiastic cheers, which lasted some
minutes*] If there is a moment of darkness and of doubt sur-

rounding our cause, holy as it is, by reason of any misfortune at Richmond, or by reason of the fact, that General McClellan [cheers] has been compelled to retreat for a short distance, it is only the more incumbent upon every friend of his country to rally to her support and to do whatever he can to give success to her cause, and to the brave men who are bound together upon the battle field to maintain it. We must do the President of the United States the justice to say, that upon many occasions he has done well. He has done well in overruling the infamous proclamations of Fremont and Hunter. He has done well in sustaining General McClellan against the machinations of traitors in Congress and out of Congress. [cheers] In these respects he has done very well indeed; and if he will now only put the foot of power upon the neck of Abolitionism, and hold it down under his foot [cheers] so that our soldiers may be left unembarrassed to fight the battles of our country, the Union will yet be saved. [cheers] During the whole war there has not been found a single officer who has done credit to himself in the field, who does not loathe from the bottom of his heart this foul spirit of fanaticism which has been found to be so dangerous to our cause up to the present hour. If the President will only hold the spirit of Abolitionism down [cheers] victory will very soon perch upon our banners, and the nation's flag will be carried everywhere in triumph. [enthusiastic cheers]

My friends, I shall not detain you, because there is a great deal to be offered for your enjoyment to-day. Let me add, however, that I feel assured that there is no tongue here present upon which does not falter the vow that the Constitution which is now committed to our care and keeping with our brother patriots throughout the land, shall be preserved inviolate; [loud cheers] and no heart which does not accept the sentiment, with the devotion of life itself, "That the Union of these States shall remain now and forever, one and inseparable." [loud cheers.]

THE National Hymn, "*My Country, 'Tis of Thee*," was then sung by Professor COLBURN and a chorus of twenty-four boys, accompanied on the piano by Professor CHARLES F. OLNEY.

After which GEORGE W. McLEAN, Esq., read the DECLARATION OF INDEPENDENCE, which was received with tumultuous applause, and at its termination repeated cheers were given for the "*Union*," the "*Tammany Society*," and for the reader, Col. McLEAN.

The patriotic song and chorus, "*Columbia, the Gem of the Ocean*," was then admirably sung by Professor COLBURN and his pupils.

Miss ANNIE MAHON sang a very pretty ballad written by her father, Mr. JOHN MAHON, and entitled "*A Soldier is my Beau.*" The song, in which she was assisted by the twenty-four juvenile vocalists, was warmly applauded and deservedly encored. The allusions—introduced in an additional verse—to General McCLELLAN and Col. CORCORAN were received with tremendous and repeated cheers.

Grand Sachem WATERBURY introduced HOSEA B. PERKINS, Esq., who addressed the audience as follows:

GENTLEMEN OF THE TAMMANY SOCIETY: — It has been announced that I would recite "ELIZA COOK'S ODE TO WASHINGTON." Since the announcement was made I have received from a gentleman, not unknown to literary fame, an original poem on "WASHINGTON," written for the occasion, with the request that I would submit it for your consideration. I shall be very happy to substitute it if you so desire, and it remains for you to say which of the two I shall read.

The audience, in response, called for the reading of the original poem, and Mr. PERKINS proceeded to recite the following Ode, which was loudly applauded throughout.

2

ODE TO WASHINGTON.

Of all the heroes who have shone on history's starry page,
The light, the glory, and the pride of each successive age,
Whose name's the brightest and the best? Whose fame's the dearest won?
They are thine own, imperial West, for thine is Washington!

The laurels that adorn his brow are fresh as when they grew,
For he was first in war and peace, as brave as he was true;
And from oppression's iron grasp with strong and constant hand,
He ransomed all his countrymen, and saved his native land.

In council wise, in prudence firm, and spotless in renown,
He put away ambition's prize and spurned a kingly crown.
Wealth had no lure to drag him down from his transcendent place,
For dearer than the world to him the freedom of his race!

He was the Joshua of his time—all men obeyed his will:
And in the valleys, where he fought, the sun and moon stood still.
The soldier of the Lord he went, held by a mighty hand,
Till he had passed the wilderness and reached the promised land.

No warrior of the classic roll called out a juster praise,
For Cæsar gained no grander spoils and wore no greener bays.
Like Cæsar, too, how wise he wrote, though not with blood-stained pen,
The record of the noblest deeds performed by noble men.

Great while he led his armies on—*great* while he ruled the land,
And greater yet, when he resigned his country's high command—
When, great as he had lived, he died all willing to depart,
America was found engraved upon his inmost heart.

He loved the Union—"Guard it well"—the dying hero said,
"That hour, which sees its broken bonds, will see your freedom dead.
"Oh! guard it well, and let it stand for its own sake secure,
"Then Peace, sustained by Liberty, through ages shall endure."

Alas! could he have seen the hour that we have lived to see,
He might have deeply mourned the death of Peace and Liberty.
But, could we listen to his voice, as oft it spoke before,
Our broken bonds might be rejoined, and union rise once more.

Oh! that his spirit might descend to-day, like heavenly fire,
And light upon our country's shrines the old fraternal fire :
Then love and peace might live again, and hate and war be done,
As with accordant lips we hail the name of Washington!

Professor Colburn and pupils then sang the following spirited

SONG AND CHORUS.

" The Drum-Tap Rattles Thro' the Land."

The drum-tap rattles thro' the land,
    The trumpet calls to arms,
A startled Nation stands aghast,
    Unused to war's alarms!
Ho! watchman on the outer wall!
    What danger do you see?
" To arms, to arms!" the sentry cries,
    " To arms, if you'd be free!"
Chorus—" To arms, to arms!" the sentry cries,
          " To arms if you'd be free!"

Hark! heard you not that booming gun!
    'Twas aim'd at Sumter's walls!
To arms, to arms! the cry speeds on,—
    To arms! or Freedom falls!
For on those walls our Banner floats,
    Assail'd by traitor hand;
To arms, to arms! a Nation shouts
    To arms! for Freedom stand!   To arms, &c.

They come, they come with patriot zeal,
    From workshop, store and farm;
Resolved to save their Country's Flag,
    And traitor foes disarm!
Like ocean's roar their voices swell
    From plain to mountain crag;—
Union and Liberty they cry;
    One Country and one Flag!   To arms, &c.

With gath'ring strength they onward march,
    Their Country's flag to shield;
Its starry folds they bear aloft
    On many a battle-field!
They stand as once our Father's stood,
    They scorn from foe to fly,
For Freedom and Columbia's Flag
    They conquer or they die.   To arms, &c.

God speed our noble, gallant band
    Of heroes, true and brave;
March on, march on! till o'er our land
    The Stripes and Stars shall wave!
Great God of battles—bless our cause,
    Bring Peace from War's alarms!
Protect and guide us by Thy Might,
    'Till Vict'ry crowns our Arms!   To arms, &c.

The GRAND SACHEM announced that HENRY MORFORD, Esq., would read an original poem, entitled "TAMMANY AND THE UNION."

Mr. MORFORD then proceeded to read, in a clear and distinct voice, the following poem, which, throughout, elicited tumultuous and prolonged applause.

TAMMANY AND UNION.

A PATRIOTIC POEM.

BY HENRY MORFORD.

In this hall so old and honored—filled with purpose proud and high,
Stood we, friends of the republic, on the Fourth of last July.
Twelve short months ; and yet a century seems down Time's abysses hurled,
When we mark *our* lightning progress and the history of a world.
Twelve short months—a year of changes such as ne'er the nations saw
Since creation sprung from chaos at the great primeval law.
One year past—and wide around us cannons roar and thunder drums,
For once more the Nation's Birth-day to a patriot people comes.
Flags are waving, voices bursting into words of deafening cheer,
For the nation lives—God bless it!—and its natal day is here !

One year since, and who can measure what that single year has brought
For the destinies of nations and the bursting world of thought ?
That one year has taught old Europe that the Giant of the West
Bóws to nothing less than Heaven his haughty head and nodding crest ;—
That the nation once derided for its single lust of pelf,
Means to be, ere years are many, able to defend itself!—
That the nation Russell sneered at, lying in a drowsy sleep,
Has awoke, and rolled its thunders of defiance o'er the deep.—
That the nation once so peaceful, now beneath the foeman's walls
Musters such a mighty army as no living despot calls.—
That the nation snubbed and threatened, with most base and foul intent,
When two traitors Wilkes imprisoned, taken from the English Trent,
Now compels the great admission from the cringing *London Times*—
Paid apologist of Europe for the blackest, basest crimes,—
That no nation dares oppose us if we rise to *any* deed
That the country's pride may order or its iron arm may need ;—
That if Canada we covet, and stretch out our armed hand,
England's pride and England's power cannot check the bold demand !

This from England!—from the power that through centuries old and long
Has not owned one single equal in her course of powerful wrong!—
This from England, that has girdled half the earth with bristling steel,
And down-trodden countless millions under her remorseless heel!—
This from Ireland's proud oppressor—this from India's tyrant foe—
This from her whose intermeddling helped to lay poor Poland low.
This from her who in *our* troubles would an open foe appear,
But that something cries "Forbear! it may be dangerous meddling here!"
This from her whose back and shoulders writhe in powerless rage and pain
Under those strong Union lashes dealt by bold GEORGE FRANCIS TRAIN!
This from her, who if she ever dares again invade our shore,
Finds *that last three hundred thousand ready, with a million more!*
This to *us*, her truant foundling, treated long with scorn and sneer—
Now so powerful grown, the mother stops and shrieks in guilty fear!

In that year of wondrous progress, once again Columbia's claim
To the mastery of the ocean, won by many a hero name—
Lost by France and England's bickerings, that had studded bay and coast
With such fleets of armed monsters as no age could ever boast—
This was all re-won and doubled, in *one* episode of war,
When from ERICSSON'S tried genius flashed the iron *Monitor!*
When the chance of gallant WORDEN for immortal honor came,
And he won it, sure and steady, in the battle's fiercest flame.—
When her guns the "cheese-box" thundered on the deadly Merrimac,
And the bolts herself assailing sent like peas from pop-guns back—
Then the French and English navies, pride and terror of the world,
At one blow were crushed and humbled—into yawls and cock-boats curled.
ERICSSON THE SWEDE—true genius!—after bearing shame and wrong,
Reapt at once the wide, full harvest that his soul had waited long;
And his great adopted country, fostering his inventive pride,
In *one gunboat found a navy that the world dared not deride!*

Soon the fleets of iron monsters, proof 'gainst fire, and shot, and shell,
And themselves with power to thunder out the flames and bolts of hell—
Will be guarding every harbor on our long Atlantic coast,
Bidding all the world defiance to mailed fleet or armed host;
Then, with our canals so widened that one single day it takes
To convey a fleet of Monitors from Hudson to the Lakes,
While above our battling armies and above the rebel lines
Something floats, that all the genius of this wondrous age combines.—
Something like the eye Almighty from the blue sky looking down
And discerning every movement made in country and in town,
While each motion of the foeman grows as plain as light at noon,
To McCLELLAN *in his marquee,* with the wires of Low's *balloon!*

Then, with such a watch unsleeping, on the land and on the sea,
Who will dare assault or insult the old Banner of the Free!

But the year has other omens, quite as pregnant and as true;
With the Sons of the Great Wigwam, more than all, *they* have to do.'
And on this, the nation's birth day, we must pause and look behind,
Measuring with a will determined and with patriotic mind
What have been the true relations, since this struggle first began,
Borne by every true and loyal honest democratic man?
What has Tammany, the ancient, done to aid the holy cause—
Done to free the land from treason and to win the world's applause?
Ribald tongues have dared to utter words that should be stamped at once
As the falsehood of the liar or the drivelling of the dunce,
Placing in a false position those who bear your honored name,
While for "wide-awakes" and negroes they demand the world's acclaim!
Is this just? Will you permit it on our history's page to stand
Without rising to efface it with a bold, determined hand?
Will you leave the blatant falsehood on the future's page to show?
Sure I hear the Great Tribe thunder, through their lips of war-paint, "No!"

Who have been the truly *loyal*, in this struggle to maintain
All that nerved the patriot's heart and all that fired his throbbing brain?
Was it base, black *Abolition*, with its false and treacherous heart,
That had done its share accursed in splitting North and South apart—
Was it *this* that formed the nucleus round which patriot men could cling
When they heard the note of danger and the cry of battle ring?
Had *Republicans* so managed what their place of power gave
Bitter feuds to cool and lessen and the bonds of old to save—
That on them the patriot feeling could with confidence rely
In that struggle when the country was to conquer or to die?

No! when broke the waves around us, and a strong-nerved pilot hand
Every heart in anguish prayed to bring the ship of state to land—
But one chart remained unblemished—but one chart no true man feared,
And by that and that alone the perilled vessel must be steered.
'Twas *democracy!* No insult *that* had given to North or South!
That had done no double deed and spoken with no deceitful mouth.
With it, all might yet be saved: without it, all was surely lost
As if o'er the sea of death the foundering bark already crossed!
Hands that held the helm were helpless: would the men once driven away
Lend for pity's sake their aid to battle through that fearful day?
This the question after Sumter asked, and answered fairly then,
Yet one year since, in this Wigwam, asked and answered once again!

One year since, and here beside us KENNEDY, your Sachem, stood,
Pledging for the good old Union what so soon he gave—his blood!
Stood where Sachem WATERBURY has so nobly stood to-day,
Uttering words of truth and honor that will never pass away.
One year since, and on this rostrum those who *dared* to shrink with fear
Heard the thunder tones of WALBRIDGE, for the Union ringing clear.
Tones that DALY soon will echo, as to-day he does his part,
With no *common pleas* to rouse and fire the patriotic heart,
But intending that his course shall show in conduct staunch and firm,
One of loyalty's *first judges* through his whole life's *general term!*
Will not BRADY—will not HILTON— well his arms in this support,
Keeping up the pride and honor of the *Democratic court?*

One year since, and those who wondered what in trials strange and new
Tammany the old and honored would resolve to say and do—
Heard an answer that the nation never more will dare forget—
Answer that through all our pulses thrills with pride and vigor yet :
"JACKSON'S bust is standing near us—JACKSON'S words our motto be!
As they ring across the mountains from his grave in Tennessee—
" 'Union now and Union ever, whatsoe'er be party's scope!
" 'Our best blood to save the nation, and for traitor necks, *the rope!*' "

Do ye know, oh friends and brothers, what that utterance was worth
To the destinies of millions and the dearest hopes of earth?
Do ye know how on this platform eyes were fixed o'er all the land,
Waiting till the proud Old Wigwam once should fairly *show its hand?*
Do ye know how thieves and traitors hoped to see its great knees quake,
And some faint and feeble utterance from its lips of palsy break?
Do ye know how Abolition would have given its black right arm,
Once to hear the Wigwam utter words to work it shame and harm?
Do ye know that if the utterance had that day been false or faint,
Nothing could have saved the nation from secession's evil taint ?
Tammany's voice was sorely needed—Tammany's voice the nation shook
With such thunder tones that no one ever more its will mistook !

Oh, the very *doubt* was shameful!—doubt like that which oft for life
Some half crazed and jealous husband throws upon a faithful wife !
What for years had stood a bulwark 'tween the ruin threatened wide
By the sectional disturbers swarming thick on every side—
But *Democracy, the faithful?* What, without its earnest aid.
Years ago had saved the nation being low in ruin laid ?
When had Tammany once faltered when the *Union* was at stake,
From which faithless side soever waves of fear might upward break?

Where amoug the nation's records figured men of truer soul
Than the scribes of the Old Wigwam had inscribed upon its roll?
Who could doubt that in their coffins would rebel its honored dead,
When around the council fire one word of treason should be said?
Who could doubt its true men living would cast off the very name,
If to bear it would be linking hands with Burr and Arnold's shame?

Hark! a sound even then was uttered that should chase one lingering doubt,
Thrilling all the nation's pulses as its fiery words rung out:
"Who dares touch the nation's banner, be the traitor's doom his lot!
Give him neither grace nor mercy—shoot him dead upon the spot!"
Who spoke out those words of truth that with no traitor thought would mix?
Who but Tammany's first Sachem—ever honored—JOHN A. DIX!
Who among our army leaders caught those words of patriot flame,
Laid them up, and swore to do them when the day of trial came?
Who but staunch and firm BEN BUTLER—BUTLER, of the "contraband"—
BUTLER, who has ruled New Orleans with a firm and even hand—
BUTLER, who when Mumford seized our starry flag of sacred fire,
Tore it from a public building—trampled it in rebel mire.—
Took no counsel, feared no threatening, wove no veil of legal fog,
But in sight of all the city hung the traitor like a dog!

Even then a Tammany Sachem had begun the martyr roll,
Bowing to the toils of service, though no toil could bow his *soul;*—
VOSBURGH of the gallant spirit—Vosburgh of the manly heart,
Who in all our great first rising bore a true and gallant part;
Even then was he we honored—KENNEDY, of spotless fame,
Raising up a corps of heroes that should bear the Wigwam's name.
Even then the dim perception dawned, no doubt, upon his eyes,
How from fields of patriot service noble souls to heaven rise.
In its providence his footsteps never pressed the battle plain,
But he died, as true a hero, on his bed of fever pain;
And above his lone grave standing, we behold a hero's sod,
And can trust him in the future in the hands of Freedom's God!

Gallant KENNEDY!—oh brothers of the order that he loved,
Well I know the friends who knew him cannot hear his name unmoved.
Never since the race of manhood with the dawn of time began,
Have you known a truer *friend,* or stood beside a worthier *man!*
And when base detraction's voice shall say that Tammany shames its place,
Bid the slanderer through the sod look down and see his clay-cold face,
Finding there the final answer that the world shall read with ease:
"Milksops, traitors, are not made of men who die such deaths as these!"

Nobly have they borne the banner—those who held the Tammany name,
For though Kennedy was dead, almost his peer in COGSWELL came ;
And no blows of greater vigor, ever veterans tried and tough
Struck, than struck the men *you* christened, at that butcher field, *Ball's Bluff :*
When poor BAKER, heart of iron, with a soft, persuasive tongue,
Fell, full ripe in years and honors, but oh far, by far too young ;
And when LANDER, pearl of knighthood, such as graced the olden song,
Met the wound foredoomed to slay him ere the coming days were long.
From that field the gallant COGSWELL went to fill a prison cell,
With too many of the soldiers he had loved and trained so well ;
But they bore their fate like heroes ; and of those who yet remained,
Who has seen the Tammany banner for one moment lost or stained ?

These are they who give the answer, when foul tongues the jibe renew :
"Tammany—Democracy—oh, who shall say that they are true ?"
And if Democratic leaders—democratic men, who bear
Full three-quarters of that ark which holds a nation's hope and prayer—
If they have not yet full answered all the questions malice gave
Of the faith with which they battled, all we loved to gain and save,
That assertion made by scripture well may stand the case in stead :
"They will not believe the truth though one should tell them from the dead !"

Twelve months since the word was sounded, as we looked at JACKSON's bust
And remembered how *his* vigor kept intact a nation's trust—
That until the war was ended, and the Union joined once more—
Hill to vale and vale to river—mountain top to ocean shore,—
We would never cease the struggle—never grudge our blood or gold
For the honor of the nation and the starry flag of old.
Never has that pledge been broken—no "conditions" have *we* set
To that loyalty the country needed and is needing yet.
We have claimed, and yet we claim it—that this struggle must not be
One to bind the *white* in slavery while it sets the negro free !—
We have claimed, and yet we claim it, that the sword the nation draws
Must defend the *Constitution* and ignore all "higher laws"!
We have thundered, "Down with traitors, wheresoe'er they ope the mouth—
Abolition in New England, with rebellion in the South."
We have said, "In vain this fighting, if when all the strife is done,
But the barren *soil* is conquered and no people's *hearts* are won !"
Is this *treason ?* If it be so, let the curse of ages fall,
For the democrats are traitors—rampant, dangerous traitors, *all !*

But we *shall* be traitors, mark you, when the nation calls for aid
And some democratic *Andrew* chaffers o'er it like a trade !—

Tells the government, "*So many* of our men perhaps may go,
If you shape the war to please us—bend your policy thus and so!
If you bow the knee to Hunter, let his proclamation stand
As the rule by which to govern warfare over all the land!
Do *this*, and our men we pour you, like the conquering hosts of Rome :
Act except as *we* shall bid, and Massachusetts stays at home!"
How much meaner, subtler treason could the Carolinas show,
When their black "State Rights" they preached us, in the troubles long ago?"
Every *State* to be the master—all coerce the nation's head!—
What is this but rank "secession," growing in a Northern bed?"

Honor be to ABRAHAM LINCOLN, that thus far his course is true,
Doing for the nation's welfare all an honest man can do!
Honor to his name forever, that no Abolition force
Seems to have the power to move him far from safety's middle course!
Long ago he learned the lesson that they all must learn at length—
That the black Chicago platform had no element of strength—
That republican support at best must prove a rope of sand,—
That democracy must aid him if he wished to save the land.

He has erred—for man is mortal—but few men of any age
Could have walked so well and nobly on his racked, distracted stage.
He will save the perilled nation if his better sense he heeds,
Listens to that voice of warning that the best of rulers needs,
" Puts his foot down " till it crushes all fanaticism flat,
And becomes what all can welcome—*a full-blooded democrat.*

On your strong right arm, McCLELLAN—that strong *democratic* arm,
And that brain still engineering plans to work the rebels harm—
On those plans by SCOTT once moulded, and with patience carried out,
Spite of all the yells and curses of a brainless rabble rout,—
On these all, stout GEORGE McCLELLAN, we can lean and have no fear,
Though the progress of our armies slow and tedious may appear ;
Though repulsed by thrice your numbers in the longest, deadliest fight
That e'er tested bone and muscle—brain and patriotic might—
Though *repulsed*, yet not *defeated*—no!—let Monday's, Tuesday's close,
When the lion turned at bay and rent to shreds his crowding foes,
Let these answer if you fail us in our day of sorest need!—
If you have not proved a hero worthy of our noblest meed!
Such men may be foiled a moment, but, though coward cheeks turn pale,
Victory springs from past disaster, for they are not born to fail!
Onward with the reinforcements!—onward to the rescue pour!
Richmond falls before you leave it—that we know and ask no more!

Long since had the fight been ended. but that jealousy most base,
Shedding on the time and country bitter, long and foul disgrace.
Foiled your plans and shrunk your forces, in the fear that yet some day
You might be, if *too successful, in the politicians' way !*
But the people know the story, and the people wait in hope
Till you make the foe "skedaddle" and they're "bagged" by young John Pope !
Pope—the strong right hand of Halleck. and the man the people want
'Stead of all the fuss and feathers clustered 'round the weak Fremont !
Victories yet shall crown the standard—victories scattered far and wide.
Like the long, bright roll of battles won on Mississippi's side !
Not even blunders like Manasses—like Ball's Bluff, and Charleston fight,
Where the gallant Seventy-ninth were mowed like grass. disdaining flight—
Not even these can stop the torrent, or can keep it long delayed
While the boys can use the bayonet in *Dan Sickles's brigade !*
While the Irish legions struggle, with the bravest deeds of man,
To revenge their fallen comrades and release Mike Corcoran !
Twelve months since, upon this platform, Tammany its portion chose—
"Union, truth and God forever! death to all the country's foes !"
And to-day the cry it echoes—let the patriot fight go on
Till we hold the last far stronghold—till the last red field is won !
It may cost us lives uncounted—it may cost us gold by tons,
And the country, When 'tis ended, sure must mourn her bravest sons ;
Taxes may awhile oppress us, and the languid throbs of trade
Show the great, wide desolation that the rebel hands have made ;
But for this the arms of Moses must not falter, sink and fall ;
For the *Union*—Heaven's best blessing!—oh, the *Union's* worth it *all !*

Would ye know *whose* hands are faithful and *whose* hearts are brave and true ?
Then a test to-day we bring you that the needed work may do !
In the far South-west, imprisoned, threatened, starved and almost hung
By the bitter, hopeless traitors whom his lot was cast among,
Lived a man whose name will linger while one pulse of faith we know,
As the firmest friend of Union—as secession's deadliest foe.
Some of you since then have met him—all of you well know his name,
And for brave old Parson Brownlow every true man's love we claim !
Well, released at last from bondage, free to wander where he will,
The old Parson makes his journeys. preaching Union—Union still ;
And but yesterday he published, what no true man needs to look
More than once before he buys it—known as "Parson Brownlow's Book."
And that book is dedicated to the men he loves the best—
Those whom he would clasp most warmly to his patriotic breast.
Listen to the words he utters—how he calls the noble roll
That embraces in the Union every true and loyal soul :

"To the brave man and the honest—to the patriot citizen
Ranked among the unconditional, never-faltering Union men ;—
To all those who love the loyal, and rebellion hold in scorn,
Whether in the North or South the traitor miscreant was born,
And no matter under what pretence the crime bursts out in flower—
For the sake of office, money, fame or pride, revenge or power ;—
To those men—whatever party they may honor as their own,
Who will never see their government disgraced and overthrown,
But beneath the starry banner swear to live or swear to die,
Though the prison walls are mouldy and the gallows beam is high ;
To all men who fight this battle and will perish ere they yield,
With the Union for their war-cry and its power their sword and shield!"

These are they to whom the Parson points with honor and with pride
This displays a creed beneath which North and South will ne'er divide.
'Tis an oath—all true men take it. This to be, till time is gray,
Tammany, the old and loyal, swears with upstretched arm to-day!
For the country—the whole country—still to fight till all is won!
For the Union—the *old* Union—ne'er to think our labor done !
To give freely, blood and treasure, till all's o'er or all is given,
And to hold the good old flag the dearest thing beneath the heaven!

Will red Abolition join us, in the oath that thus we swear,
For the country—the *whole* country—everything to do and dare?
No !—for when it *did*, its mission to disturb the public peace
And make foes of friends and brothers,—with the very word would cease !
Till it does so, blight and palsy fall upon his coward name
Who would bow to please a *faction* and brand *national men* with shame !

Through long years of pride and honor, spite of all that else befel,
Democratic counsels bore us—ever safely, ever well.
When they failed, the land was perilled : when once more they rule the hour,
Treason will be dead and buried and rebellion hurled from power!
Labor all, by word and ballot, for that glorious coming day
When all sectional disturbance shall be dead and swept away—
When no other aspiration any man shall *dare* to draw
Than "God save the good old Union—Constitution, love and law !"

Brothers!—'tis the Nation's Birth-day, honored o'er the whole broad land
Where the fatal curse, secession, has not laid its blighting hand.
Pray with me that yet another anniversary we may keep
Long before one man amongst us falls in death's unbroken sleep—
Anniversary of that morning, soon to be, if God is just,
When the last secession army kneels for peace or bites the dust,—
When the good old flag from Sumter once again in pride is flung,
With the last poor wanderer pardoned, and the last arch-rebel *hung !*

Professor COLBURN and pupils then sang the following

CHORUS--PATRIOTIC HYMN --" FOREVER."

WORDS BY NELSON J. WATERBURY.   MUSIC BY GEO. F. BRISTOW.

GOD bless our own dear land ;
Its sons together band,
　　　Forever and forever.
From ocean unto ocean,
Inspire but one emotion,
One hope and one devotion.
　　　God bless our country ever,
　　　Forever and forever.

God bless our Union chain,
Each sacred link retain,
　　　Forever and forever:
With other links extend it,
Let treason never rend it,
From every foe defend it.
　　　God bless the Union ever,
　　　Forever and forever.

God bless our banner bright,
The Standard of the Right,
　　　Forever and forever ; .
Its Stripes and Constellation,
Our hearts' fond adoration,
The glory of our nation,
　　　God bless that Flag forever,
　　　Forever and forever.

God bless the homes we love,
And guard them from above,
　　　Forever and forever.
The angel lips which pray there,
The little ones who play there,
The manly hearts that sway there—
　　　God bless them all forever,
　　　Forever and forever.

After the singing of an original patriotic ballad by Mr. FRANK O'DONNELL, the Grand Sachem introduced the Orator of the day— Hon. CHARLES P. DALY—first Judge of the Court of Common Pleas, who was most enthusiastically received. When silence was restored, Judge DALY addressed the vast and attentive audience as follows:

ORATION.

BY HON. CHARLES P. DALY.

IT is now, fellow-citizens, exactly three hundred years ago this year, and at this present season of the year, since the first settlement was made in the United States. In that year, 1562, a small squadron of ships, containing a body of French Huguenot adventurers, entered the harbor of Port Royal, for the purpose of colonization and settlement. On one of the islands, now in possession of the Federal troops, and over which the flag of the Union now waves, twenty-six of these adventurers built a fort and established a settlement, raising a monumental stone inscribed with the arms of France and giving to the country the name of Carolina. After three centuries have elapsed from this first attempt at occupation and settlement of what, since the 4th of July, 1776, has been known as the United States,—three centuries which have witnessed a tide of ceaseless emigration, ultimately leading to a powerful nation under the government of democratic institutions, we have beheld upon this very soil of Carolina, the development of a spirit that would destroy the structure it has cost centuries to erect, and which has leagued in its suicidal policy, the feeblest, the least enlightened, and the most aristocratic, of those hitherto living under a common government. During these three hundred years, our story may be briefly told in the fact, that in the first two centuries and a quarter we increased in population but to four millions, and that in the three-quarters of a century that has elapsed since the formation of the Constitution of the United States we have swelled to the magnitude of thirty millions. The first two centuries is a history of colonial vassalage, in which we were controlled by the government of England, and deeply impregnated with the ideas, forms, and aristocratic notions of society, growing out of monarchial institutions.

The first quarter of the remaining century was spent in effecting our independence and afterward in a hopeless attempt to get on as independent sovereignties, under a compact by which each State bound itself, as expressed in the articles of the Confederation, " to assist each other against all force offered to, or attack made upon them, or any of them on account of religion, sovereignty, trade, or any other pretence, whatever." We were a cluster of nationalities and not a nation. That event commenced with the adoption of the Constitution, which, discarding the old terms that denoted a league of States, opened with the expressive words, " We, the people of the United States." From that period we have presented a spectacle of gigantic growth in population, arts, industry, wealth and territory, under a democratic national government, such as has never been witnessed during the same space of time in the history of mankind under any form of government.

Knit together by the geographical relation of each part to the whole, by the lines which nature has marked in mountain chains, in the direction and confluence of great rivers, and in our wide expanse of sea coast, we have added to the advantages of nature by an internal web of railroads, and through our energetic industry have brought about a combination of interests, agricultural, commercial, mechanical, and manufacturing, so closely interwoven as to make that of the one dependent upon that of the other. Isolated from the nations of the old world, and almost equally separated from the Southern Hemisphere by the waters of the Gulf of Mexico, we have an exemption from the dangers of foreign conquest or aggression to which nations less fortunately situated are subject.

Such *was* the spectacle we have hitherto presented. We had nothing to fear but ourselves: and now on this third centennial anniversary of our beginning as a people, we assemble on this day, so sacred in our annals, with the consciousness that a blow has been struck at the fabric we have reared, so sudden and so powerful in its effect as to show the existence of deep-seated causes, which it has now become our duty as men and as patriots to consider.

Our government is that of a Democracy, with limitations and features however that distinguish it from that of any government of a similar kind that has ever existed. We did not derive it from the political teachings of speculative writers; but it grew up from our own wants, necessities, and mutual dependence upon each other during the long period of our colonization and settlement. It was the necessary and natural result of causes operating in the first period of our history, and is the only form of government under which we could, or can advance as a people. This is a truth expressed in the axiom of MONTESQUIEU, "that every people must be developed according to the laws of their origin."

It may not be the best fitted for other nations, but it is the only one that is adapted to us. It is susceptible of modifications, of changes, and of many improvements, but in its fundamental principles it must go on, the result in the great future being its permanent establishment as a successful form of human government, or anarchy. Certain things have taken deep root and have become so incorporated in our habits, opinions and laws as to have to us the significance of truth. We have had strong faith in the wisdom and good sense of the multitude, and believe that though often mistaken and carried away, they will come in the end to the right conclusion; that they are on the whole the best judges of their own interests, and that it is safer and better to trust in them than to any exclusive and aristocratic class constituted to rule over and direct them. That to that end everything should be done for the education of the people; that they cannot be too much enlightened, and that general education and unrestricted freedom in every department of human labor will produce great intellectual and material development, gradually elevating the mass and improving the physical, intellectual and moral condition of the whole people. That the effect of republican institutions is to make men rely more upon themselves and to call into greater activity their intellectual and industrial qualities. That an aristocratic class, however refined or cultivated in itself, tends rather to retard than to advance the condition of the whole people, and that consequently every thing which tends to perpetuate property in families should in this country be restricted as leading to a class that produces nothing while it arrogates to itself an assumed superiority based upon the distinction of family.

Whether we are right or wrong in these ideas; whether it is possible or not to carry them out, we have been earnestly engaged in the attempt for a period now of eighty-six years, and whether it be wise or not, considered in respect to our perpetuity as a nation, it is at least a fact, that under no government which has previously existed, has the mass of the people ever enjoyed the same amount of material comforts, felt the same degree of personal independence, or shared so largely in the creation of the laws by which they are governed. These ideas, now working out in practical development, have penetrated to the depths of European society, and attracted to our shores men of all nationalities, dissatisfied with the governments under which they lived, and making this country their own by the deliberate act of adoption. This never-ceasing tide has gone on adding to our material wealth and productive industry, and keeping up that attrition, rough contact, and collision of interests which must exist where there is a gradual uprising and elevation of the masses. In a state of transition like this there is very little that is attractive to the admirers of European society, and hence, all of this class, from Mrs. TROLLOPE, to Mr. RUSSELL, of the *London Times*, have agreed in disliking the country; but to

4

the poor man, battling in the great struggle of life, seeking to improve the condition of himself and family, this broad territory, under the development of democratic institutions, has presented a home such as he has never found since the world began; and that he so feels and understands it is manifest in the multitude of men, both native and foreign, who have voluntarily left their peaceful, industrial pursuits, to maintain with their lives the institutions under which these blessings have been enjoyed.

Whilst such has been the result in the Northern States, a very different state of things has prevailed in the States of the South. Agricultural in their interests, the labor there, which is the productive source of their wealth, is performed by a servile class, and as a necessary consequence of the existence of the relation of master and serf, society there is and must be more aristocratic in its developments. The pride of birth, the distinction of family, and the possession of refined and cultivated manners, are there what is most valued, as well by those who possess them as by those who do not. There the tide of European emigration has never flowed, the field of labor being exclusively occupied and society constituted upon a basis of slavery which cannot be lightly disturbed, nor changed nor altered with any good result, except by measures to be administered alone by the people among whom it exists. It is the tendency of an aristocracy to give special importance to everything pertaining to themselves: and the aristocracy of two of the oldest of the Southern States—South Carolina and Virginia—exalt themselves especially over what they call their blood and descent: the one as the descendants of the Huguenots, and the other of the Cavaliers. It is not much matter, in a contest like this, how, or from whom, they are descended; but as they speak of themselves as a *high-souled* race, descended from a stock wholly different from the "*mud-sills*," as they term the masses of the North, and give that as a reason why they cannot be tied to its rough and vulgar democracy, it may be as well to see upon what authority this claim to distinguished descent rests, and to settle it by an appeal to history.

The first Huguenots who settled in Carolina are described by the historian as "a motley group of dissolute men, mad with a passion for sudden wealth, among whom mutinies were frequent, and who commenced their career by a course of piracy against the Spaniards," and the inhabitants of this province kept up a course of piratical enterprises which almost annihilated commerce in the American seas in the latter part of the seventeenth century. CHALMERS in his annals says, "The Governor of Carolina, the proprietary deputies, the principal inhabitants, all degraded themselves to a level with the meanest of mankind by assisting pirates, and by receiving the plunder of nations." Nor was their disgrace the only inconvenience which resulted from their infamous conduct: but their long-continued troubles with the Spaniards in Florida grew out of the indignation with which that people saw the plunderers of their wealth openly encouraged at Charleston. How completely they had devoted themselves to this mode of life, may be inferred from a letter from WHITCHELL, April 10th, 1684, to the Governor, Deputies, and Council of Carolina, suggesting "that the opening of a trade by the colony with the Spaniards might induce a more honest mode of enriching themselves, than by plundering his Majesty's allies." And in keeping with this state of society there was no administration of the ordinances of religion in Carolina for many years after its establishment as a colony.

A single authority will suffice, as respects Eastern Virginia, to show who were the ancestors of those who constitute the present chivalry of that rebellious part of the State, Western Virginia having been settled by emigrants from the north of Ireland. That authority comes from the highest source; an eye witness, the celebrated Captain JOHN SMITH, whose name is so inseparably interwoven with the poetical story of POCAHONTAS. He describes the settlers of Eastern Virginia in these words, which are not altogether inapplicable even at the present day. "A great part" he says, "were unruly sparks, packed off by their friends to escape worse destinies at home. Many were poor gentlemen, broken tradesmen, rakes, libertines, footmen, and such others as were much fitter to spoil and ruin a commonwealth than to help to raise or to maintain one." To which may be added, that these two colonies received in larger proportion than any of the rest, the transported convicts of England. This is history, and with these facts on the page of history how ridiculous is this assumption of distinguished descent. It is best disposed of in the memorable lines of POPE :

> " Count me those only who were good and great,
> Go ! if your ancient but ignoble blood,
> Has only crept through scoundrels since the flood ;
> Go ! and pretend your family is young,
> Nor own your fathers have been fools so long.
> What can ennoble slaves, or sots, or cowards,
> Alas ! not all the blood of all the Howards."

The transition from pride of birth and of family to State pride is only an expansion of the same passion. Hence in these States, especially in the older ones, we have had the most extravagant pretensions put forth under the title of "State Rights." Such was the claim of nullification by which South Carolina arrogated to herself the right of nullifying any law of the general government which did not please her, and latterly the doctrine of peaceable secession, of which she was the parent. This peculiarity existed as early as the revolution. The chief difficulty then was to get the aristocratic States of the South to unite with the others in the effort to separate from Great Britain. JOHN ADAMS wrote to General GATES, on the 23d March, 1776, in these words, "All our misfortunes arise from a single source—the reluctance of the Southern colonies to a Republican government." And before the adoption of the Constitution. Washington, knowing their restlessness under rule, their high estimate of their own importance, and that they had interests peculiar and different from the other States, gave some advice to the whole country, the wisdom of which, if not previously appreciated, is now painfully apparent. " We are," he said in the Summer of 1785, "either an united people, or thirteen independent sovereignties, eternally counteracting each other. If the former, then, whatever such a majority of the States as the Constitution points out, conceives to be for the benefit of the whole, it should be submitted to by the minority. Let the Southern States be always represented, let them act more in union, let them declare freely and boldly what is for their interest, and what is prejudicial to them, and there will be, there must be, an accommodating spirit." Edmund Burke, one of the profoundest of statesmen and the ablest of writers upon government that England has produced, has declared that the vital principle in the practical working of a free government is *compromise*. It has been our heavy misfortune to live in an age when this great truth has been scouted by superficial journalists, fulsome orators, and political parsons, who, unitedly, have had influence enough to build up a party that has carried this thriving and prosperous country into one of the most extended and complicated civil wars that has ever taken place upon the face of this globe. The unexampled growth of this nation under influences so opposed to the fixed views of nearly every other existing government, was a spectacle to invoke every species of unfavorable comment on the part of unfriendly observers and writers. We commenced our government amid the predictions of Englishmen of every rank that the whole affair would immediately tumble to pieces, and when that was falsified by our amazing progress, the inconsistency between our political principles and our practice, as exhibited in the institu-

tion of slavery, was seized upon and has been a choice theme
for the last thirty years for English writers, journalists, orators
and travellers.

It would have been well had we imitated our censors, the
English, in their indifference to the opinions of other nations.
We have imitated them in a quality in which they especially
excel, the art of blowing their own trumpet; but we have particularly in New England, exhibited a sensitiveness to everything that an Englishman was pleased to utter upon the subject
of slavery, very unlike the indifference with which Englishmen
heard that their countrymen in India· had taken prisoners of
war and by way of example blown them into fragments from
the mouths of cannon. It is the infirmity of many of our New
England brethren to look only upon one side of a question: to
collect with untiring industry everything which tends to justify
that and to treat with contempt everything opposed to it. This
is especially illustrated in the way in which they have looked
upon our national interests in its connection with the subject of
slavery. What *they* think others must think. This class of
men in New England are as little tolerant in matters of opinion as their ancestors were two hundred years ago, and as men
of the same stamp then did not hesitate to burn the witch and
the unrecanting Quaker, so among the modern abolitionists men
are found ready to counsel the slave to fire the dwelling of his
master, and give him, his wife and his children to the flames.
It also happens that the Southern Puritan, the descendant of the
Huguenot, resembles very much in this respect his Eastern
brother. On the subject of slavery he will tolerate no opinion
but his own. With him it is the key-stone of the social edifice.
the only basis upon which civil society can rest, the structure
upon which to rear a higher form of civilization, views of which
he has become as active a propagandist.throughout the South, as
his Eastern antagonist has been in the North of his pet scheme

of immediate emancipation. For some time the Eastern pro-pagandist gave himself to the task of convincing the South of the sinfulness and moral iniquity of slavery, and the necessity for its immediate abolition, and it ended, as might have been expected, in both becoming more firmly convinced in the correct-ness of their own views than before. The next remedy was political agitation, violent denunciation of the South, its people and institutions, and precisely in proportion as that increased did the South doggedly determine to make slavery a lasting and perpetual thing.

The great Democratic party, true to the instincts which, for fifty years, have preserved and guided it as an organization looking to the welfare of the *whole* country, opposed itself as a barrier, and was able to do so successfully until the *South de-serted* it, and it was borne down by the surging tide of the Re-publican party. Abraham Lincoln was elected according to the mode prescribed by the Constitution, a result waited for by the South as the signal for the breaking up of the government. The work of dismemberment began. *What* was the duty of the Democratic party, then? *Powerless* as a political minority, it pressed BURKE'S remedy (compromise),—the remedy which Eng-land has successfully employed in political agitations as violent and as threatening as this, and by which HENRY CLAY had be-fore steadied the disturbed bark of the State. Its voice was unheeded. The triumphant Republicans would neither believe in the possibility of separation, nor in the danger of civil war. Mr. GREELEY declared that the South were so dependent upon the North that "it could not be kicked out of the Union;" and even when every arsenal in the South had been seized, and ten thousand men beleaguered Sumter, the Government was more beset and taken up by the clamorous appeals for office than by the perilous condition of the country.

When the culminating blow was at last struck, no one asked

what was the duty of the Democratic party then. It was anti-
cipated by the impulsive action of its masses—by the crowds of
Democrats who filled the ranks of the regiments, and who now
constitute the two-thirds of the army of the Union. Fortunately for the Government an honest man was found at its head,
determined to stand by the Constitution, and enforce it as long
as the people would stand by him. We have now been involved
over a year in this war. We have already incurred, in conduct-
ing it, an expense equal to one-fourth of the national debt of
Great Britain, and to every man who is able to think for himself it is manifest that we have not yet reached the heart of the
rebellion. We have a task upon us equivalent to the conquest
of a nation, and in a country where the difficulties of carrying
on an offensive war, are unusually great. There is no alterna-
tive now, but to go on and prosecute the war to the utmost ex-
tent of our ability. Whatever can be accomplished, can be accomplished only by military means, for any propositions now for
a settlement would be treated by the South with contempt and
scorn. All hope or expectation of union feeling in any place
not permanently held by our troops may be abandoned. It does
not exist, or if it does, is so controlled that it will not be dis-
covered, until we have conquered their armies, and obtained
possession of their forts and cities. The work before us is a
vast one, and to accomplish it sacrifices must be undergone of
which we have at present but an inadequate conception. We
have had a call made upon the Government to raise three hundred thousand more troops. It is a wise measure; wise, not
only as a means of completing the war rapidly, but as the most
effective means of preventing the armed intervention of England and France, or of one of them, of which we stand every
moment in danger. At a crisis so critical as this, what is the
spectacle presented at Washington? The attention of Congress
absorbed in the creation of a tariff for the benefit of manufac-

turers, so sweeping in its prohibitions, as to cut off all hope of revenue, and establish a Chinese non-intercourse between us and the commercial nations of the world; and plans to effect the conquest of the South by the magical operation of confiscation bills, and for the liberation of slaves that are not in our possession. In addition to which we have politicians controlling the movements of generals, and representatives of the people who have no hesitation in declaring their intention to embarrass the Government unless it avow and act upon the policy of making this a war for the immediate emancipation of the slaves of the South; that unless that is done, they will compel the Government to consent to a separation. Let no such man talk hereafter of Southern traitors. He is, to carry out his own insane project, as ready to destroy the Government of his fathers as they. Slavery must be left to take care of itself; to bide whatever fate may attend it under the contingencies and necessities of the war. Every other consideration must be merged in the great duty of maintaining the authority of the Government by force of arms.

As the time is approaching when the Democratic party can give expression to its sentiments, it will be for them to demand that this war shall *not* be carried on as a political speculation, but as a great national work. DE TOCQUEVILLE, while declaring thirty years ago, that what he saw here convinced him of the superiority of a free government over others, at the same time pointed out what he looked upon as our greatest danger, the tendency of our political machinery to elevate to the important places of public trust, men with little or no qualification for the positions they undertake to fill. He said that we were not yet sufficiently alive to the fact that there is a certain cultivation which can never be shared by the masses, but which is essential in those who undertake to administer the affairs of a State. We have a melancholy proof of this in many of the men who now exercise an influence upon the administration of our national affairs at Washington—men dictating, with all the confidence of ignorance in a crisis like this, what should or should not be done, even in the operation of the armies. If we would preserve this government, our standard of public men must be a higher one, and it lies with the Democratic party, as the great conservator of the best interests of the nation, to look to it. The principles of republican government are on trial in this great contest. Upon us has fallen the responsibility of preserving it, and it remains to be seen whether we are or are not equal to the emergency. Other great nations have passed through the ordeal of civil war, and come out of it more strongly cemented than before. Such has been the case in England, in France, and in Spain, but in no similar instance have two great parts of a country been arrayed against each other as in this. The question may be asked, why not let them go? The answer is, that it is to give up the most important part of our country, geographically—the mouths of our commanding rivers, our national outlets, and nearly the whole of our sea-coast, leaving us but a fragment of the territory of our once great republic, so loosely connected geographically, and with interests so conflicting, that the dismemberment and breaking up of what would be left to us, would be the inevitable consequence. Look upon the map of the United States and see the nature and relative position of the country that would remain. It would be impossible for it to hold together. We must be what we have been or we are nothing. We are engaged in a struggle for national existence, and trite as it is, the watchword throughout the land must be, the Union *now* and *forever, one* and *inseparable.*

After a fantasia and variations on the piano by Mr. Sullivan,

Hon. DANIEL E. DELAVAN, proposed the following resolutions, which were unanimously adopted:

Resolved, That the Tammany Society, and its friends assembled here to-day, present their sincere thanks to the Hon. CHARLES P. DALY, for his able and patriotic oration; also to HENRY MORFORD, Esq., for the very happy original poem written and delivered by him; also to HOSEA B. PERKINS, Esq., for his impressive recitation of an original ode to Washington; also to Miss ANNIE MAHON, for the beautiful song sung by her; also to GEORGE W. McLEAN, Esq., for reading the Declaration of Independence; also to Prof. MARCUS COLBURN, and the twenty-four boys assisting him, for their fine patriotic songs and hymns; also to Prof. CHARLES F. OLNEY, for his accompaniment on the piano; also to the CECILIAN BRASS BAND, for the beautiful music played by them; also to FRANK B. O'DONNELL, Esq., for the original patriotic song composed and sung by himself; also to THOMAS D. SULLIVAN, for the fantasia and variations played by him on the piano; also to Messrs. LIGHTE and BRADBURYS, for the loan of the magnificent piano-forte used on this occasion; and further—

Resolved, That the whole proceedings of this celebration be published in pamphlet form, to be distributed to members of this Society, and to their friends.

General HIRAM WALBRIDGE then presented himself, and was received with loud and continued cheers. He said: I have, sir, a resolution to propose, which I will read:

Whereas, The United States are engaged in suppressing a wicked and infamous rebellion, against the integrity of the Constitution and the stability of the Union; and,

Whereas, continued intimations reach us of foreign intervention; The Democracy of the city and county of New York, while commemorating the anniversary of the birth of our National existence, unanimously declare:

First, That it has ever been the policy of the people and Government of the United States, to refrain from any interference in the internal conflicts of foreign powers; that this policy, early inaugurated by WASHINGTON, conceived in wisdom, and steadily maintained by patriotism and sound policy, has secured the assent and become the doctrine of the whole American people.

Second, That, if in conflict with this wide and beneficent policy, any intervention in the domestic troubles of the United States be meditated by any of the European Powers, they must count the cost of war with a spirited and independent people, with a million of men already called to the field, with an interest in the soil, and justly recognizing that the cause of republican representative government, as developed and illustrated in our institutions, has been confided in part to their sacred keeping.

Third, That the announcement of this intervention, in an authoritative form, will be no less than to sow the Northern section of this hemisphere with the fabled dragon's teeth, and, in due time, will bring forth its full crop of armed men.

The General proceeded : One year ago, to-day, standing in this place as the representative of this Society, I announced to this people the necessity of calling to the field six-hundred thousand troops.

A Voice: "So you did, I heard that."

General WALBRIDGE:. A year has transpired and Tammany has been vindicated. At that time it was asserted by many that the Gulf of Mexico would be nothing else than a European lake. Already they are attempting · to force upon this country violations of the MONROE doctrine — a doctrine which is so essential to its safety. As Tammany has been vindicated by the events of last year, I desire that these Resolutions should pass, in order to see whether the masses of this country will not vindicate our action to day. [*hear, hear and cheers*] If war must come, I desire that it shall be forced upon us by those across the water, and then we will appeal, I presume, to the courage and integrity of every man on this continent, and settle all questions. [*loud cheers*]

Ex. Grand Sachem ELIJAH F. PURDY, in seconding the adoption of the Resolutions, expressed his desire that they should be included in the Official Report of the day's proceedings.

The Resolutions were then unanimously adopted.

After the singing of the "*Star Spangled Banner*," which terminated the regular order of exercises in the large room, the assemblage, preceded by the Sachems and Officers of the Society, with their invited guests, marched in procession to

"THE BANQUET ROOM,"

where a fine collation had been prepared. After full justice had been done to the viands, champagne, punch, &c., &c., Grand Sachem WATERBURY announced the first regular toast:

THE DAY WE CELEBRATE:

> May the clouds which darken its eighty-sixth anniversary be speedily dispelled, and the sunlight of peace again gladden every part of our widely extended land.

To respond to this toast, the GRAND SACHEM said, I will introduce a gentleman whom you all know and honor; who has been absent from this country for several months, and whom I am now glad to welcome back to our shores, as I am sure you all are. I call upon the Hon. AUGUST BELMONT. [*loud cheers*]

Mr. BELMONT then presented himself, and was most warmly received. He said:

MR. GRAND SACHEM AND GENTLEMEN:

I am extremely obliged to you for the high honor you bestow upon me and the cordiality with which you welcome me home. I am deeply impressed and entirely taken by surprise; however, I thank you from the bottom of my heart. I have been absent from my country for the last ten months, compelled to a temporary residence abroad by illness in my family. It was a source of heartfelt regret for me to be away from home and from my friends in their dark hour of trial. [*cheers*] I cannot describe to you the anxiety and sorrow with which I watched the progress of our gallant army and navy; but when I saw from month to month the energy and patriotism of our people rise stronger and higher under every adversity, anxieties were relieved and my fervent hopes and conviction in the ultimate reconstruction of the Union confirmed. [*loud cheers*]

I come home at a dark and gloomy moment of the struggle in which we are engaged. It seems as if Providence had decreed this momentary reverse of our heroic army in order to admonish us on this anniversary of our National Independence, that it will require the whole energy of our people if we mean to leave to our children the blessed inheritance bestowed by the fathers of our Republic. We have to deal with a powerful enemy, arrayed in relentless strife against our institutions and the best interests of humanity, and it will require the undivided and gigantic efforts of our united people to save our country and our Union. [*loud cheers*]

There is no sacrifice too great, none which we should not most cheerfully make in order to help the government at this moment. We want more troops, more money, and everything good and loyal citizens can give to their country in this hour of danger. [*cheers*]

Allow me, Mr. Chairman, to conclude by giving the following sentiment:

"Our country, the object of our dearest affections: may she ever find her sons worthy of her, and ready to sacrifice their lives and their treasure in her defence, against domestic traitors or foreign foes." [*loud, and continued cheers*]

Grand Sachem WATERBURY, then gave the second regular toast, and said that he would call upon Judge HILTON to respond. [*cheers*]

GEORGE WASHINGTON:

Under whose paternal guidance our freedom was secured, and our country established. Universal fidelity to his precepts and example will preserve both, forever.

Hon. HENRY HILTON, who was enthusiastically received, responded to the toast in the following terms:

MR. CHAIRMAN AND FELLOW CITIZENS:

The name of WASHINGTON is one endeared to us all. It is identified with our existence as a nation, and with all that is great and good in our early history. Indeed, it may be said that from him we have sprung as a people, and to him is justly due that affectionate name of "Father of our Country." [*loud cheers*] He it was that led us through all our early trials and dangers, labored for us in our revolution, and finally brought us to victory and prosperity. [*cheers*] Through the subduing force of his mind, and his never-failing wisdom, he enabled us to emerge from a dependent existence as a colony, to a great nation, and finally to become a republic of free men. It may then justly be said of him, that under his paternal guidance our freedom was secured, and our country established. May the walls of Old Tammany always resound with words of reverence and affection for his great name. [*cheers*] May his memory, with that of JEFFERSON and JACKSON, ever be talismanic within this Hall. [*cheers*] And may the day we now celebrate be ever regarded as commemorative of the blessings which have descended to us from the services of him who was "first in war, first in peace, and first in the hearts of his countrymen." [*loud cheers*]

The Grand Sachem then gave the third regular toast:

THOMAS JEFFERSON:

His early pen traced the living words that declared our Independence; and his later writings, as approaching death quickened his vision and intensified his love, implored his countrymen to avoid the dangers of sectional strife. May his words of inspiration and warning recall the madness of treason and fanaticism, and fire anew the heart of patriotism.

General H. WALBRIDGE being called upon to respond, was

welcomed with loud and repeated applause; when silence was restored, he spoke as follows:

FELLOW CITIZENS AND FRIENDS:—There is profound wisdom at this period in the history of the Republic, when foreign intervention is said to be imminent, in recalling, even amid our thick thronging domestic disasters, the words, the writings, and the memory of the illustrious citizen and statesman, THOMAS JEFFERSON. [*hear, hear, and cheers*] In that first administration referred to by the distinguished gentleman who has just concluded—the administration of the illustrious WASHINGTON, when he was organizing the Federal Government, and shaping its policy, so as to command the respect of the generations that were to follow, he called to his support, as Secretary of State, THOMAS JEFFERSON, who brought to the discharge of the high duties confided to him, great and commanding ability, an unselfish patriotism, profound learning as a publicist, with vast research, and unimpeachable integrity. [*loud cheers*] Our relations with England, were still of an unsatisfactory character. The drama of the French Revolution was about to startle and astonish the Christian world. We had previously formed a treaty of alliance with the French nation, who had materially aided us in the struggles of the Revolution. France had determined to send forth her hitherto invincible legions in search of conquest through Continental Europe. England, her great rival, had dominion upon the sea, but the earth trembled beneath the advancing tread of the heroic French. It became a question of grave complications, and serious import, whether our treaty with France rendered it obligatory on the part of the American people to engage in her aggressive designs. It is not too much to say, the destiny of our free institutions was involved in the decision. The country turned with anxious solicitude to the decision of WASHINGTON. He comprehended, not only the high responsibility resting upon him, but the vast consequences in-

volved. WASHINGTON determined to steer clear of all foreign
complications, and to avoid taking part in the strife that was
to deluge Europe with blood. [*cheers*] The Secretary of
State was authorized to enunciate to the world the American
doctrine of neutrality, in all foreign disputes. THOMAS JEF-
FERSON rose adequate to the occasion. He had, in 1776, framed
the declaration that severed the connection of the colonies from
Great Britain. A duty equally sublime was now confided to
him, *to prescribe the policy of the new government in its intercourse
with foreign powers.* THAT POLICY WAS DECLARED TO BE NON-
INTERVENTION IN THE INTERNAL CONFLICTS OF FOREIGN STATES.
[*cheers.*]

This doctrine, then first proclaimed by a young and rising
nation, has become the recognized and acknowledged doctrine
of all civilized states. To the immortal honor of the American
people—be it forever said—they determined, on the soil of this
new hemisphere, they would lay broad and deep the founda-
tions of free institutions, without desiring to interfere in the
collisions of other States. [*loud cheers*]

From that hour to this, we have invariably pursued this wise,
just, and beneficent policy, nor have we departed from it when
revolution and tumults have ruled throughout the British Empire,
at different intervals, from Canada to India; we have pursued
the same undeviating policy, even when Ireland was struggling
to regain her long lost nationality, though our keenest sympa-
thies were stimulated with gratitude for the heroic devotion
with which many of her cherished sons fell fighting for American Independence. [*loud and continued cheering*]

When, therefore, we are engaged in a domestic dissension—
when a portion of our misguided citizens have raised the banner of revolt and rebellion against the Federal authority, and
against that very Constitution which guaranteed them every
protection, it is a deep and burning shame, a monument of eter-

nal infamy for any power from across the water to involve themselves, by any intervention, in our present domestic struggle.
[*cheers.*] It is in direct conflict with the policy we have
ourselves hitherto pursued, and which policy secured for us the
regard of the whole christian world. BUT I SHALL NOT DESPAIR.
IF THIS FOREIGN INTERVENTION IS TO COME, I REPEAT IT, LET IT
COME. There is a God in heaven. There is a power that deals
out justice among nations as among men, and if, in violation of
all honor and all law, any armed intervention from abroad is
to be imposed upon this great, loyal American people, relying
upon our own strong arm, we will implore the God of battles to
smile upon us, as upon our fathers in the darkened period of the
Revolution, and we will enter upon the contest, determined
that here liberty shall build her last entrenchment, and that
we shall fight till we spill the last drop of our blood in
maintaining and preserving, free, representative, constitutional
government, from the grasping avarice or ambition of any
foreign invaders. [*cheers*] In such a conflict, the loyal, true
men of America will be sustained by the genuine lovers of
freedom in both hemispheres. [*long and protracted applause*]

The Grand Sachem next gave the fourth regular toast:

THE UNION:

> The glorious arch that spans our national horizon; may no
> pleiad ever be lost from its constellation.

Mr. HENRY L. CLINTON briefly responded: After the electri-
fying words which they had just heard from the distinguished
gentleman who had last addressed them, he (Mr. C.) felt that
nothing he could say, would add to the importance of the sentiment, or to the occasion. While the previous speaker (WAL-
BRIDGE) was addressing them, he (Mr. C.) could not but reflect,
with joyous satisfaction, that there was one *bridge* representing

the democratic strength, over which, neither domestic traitors, nor insolent foreign interventionists, in their mad designs to crush this country, could ever pass; and that *bridge* was old Tammany's *Wal*BRIDGE. [*cheers*] Let England or France, or any number of foreign nations assail us, and they will find us a nation of *Wal-bridges*, provided with invincible and eternal barriers to all foreign intervention in our domestic affairs. [*loud and continued cheers.*] There was but one sentiment interwoven in the thoughts, and stamped in characters of glowing fire upon the heart of this great nation, which was embraced in the words of the sainted hero whose portrait fitly decks the walls of Tammany : "The Union must and shall be preserved." [*loud cheering*] While our beloved country was wrapt in the flames of civil strife, while the evils of the worst of all wars--a civil war-- overspread the land, it was no small consolation for every firm and consistent democrat to reflect that the democratic party had done all in its power to avert the dreadful catastrophe. He (Mr. C.) believed in the most determined and energetic prosecution of the war. After some further remarks in regard to the incalculable benefits of the Union, and the ruin of the country's dearest interests, which would follow in the wake of dissolution, Mr. C., in conclusion said : Let us ever fight for and protect to the last extremity, the glorious old ship of state. May she ever be preserved to us, undecayed by time, unharmed by man. For over eighty years, freighted with liberty's choicest blessings, with the nation's dearest interests, with the hopes of the civilized world, she has carried us in safety over the troubled waters of the political deep. But if, in the providence of God, she shall ever be destined to founder--to sink—let our last lingering gaze be upon the glorious old flag--the stars and stripes --nailed to the mast; let the last sound which breaks on our ear be, the consecrated words, "*Dont give up the ship*". [*loud cheers.*]

The Grand Sachem gave the fifth regular toast:

THE CONSTITUTION:

> Its power, which is enforced even at the point of the bayonet,
> shall be a shield to the rights of every citizen, and to the
> rights of every State.

Hon. RICHARD B. CONNOLLY, in presenting himself to respond to the toast, was received with hearty and repeated cheers. He said:

FELLOW DEMOCRATS: I have been called upon by the Grand Sachem to respond to the toast of "The Constitution." If I had the eloquence of a Walbridge, I might do justice to that toast, but being an humble, unpretending individual myself, unaccustomed to public speaking, I can only let my heart pour forth a few plain words in response to that glorious toast. [*cheers.*] This is the day which is hallowed by the memory of the man who made that Constitution, and in these trying times every man who loves liberty as well as his life, should stand up in support of that Constitution, which is giving to every man, no matter how humble he may be, in this great country, equal privileges with the rich and powerful in the land. [*hear, hear, and loud cheers.*] That Constitution, fellow democrats, is now on its trial. Two great armies are in hostile array engaged in fighting for that Constitution, one fighting for the great principles laid down in that Constitution, and the other desiring to trample it in the dust. [*cheers*] And all I hope is, and I pray to Almighty God, that victory will perch upon the banner of that army which is fighting for the Constitution of the United States, and fighting for life and liberty. [*loud cheers*] In these trying times let us abandon all party, and let us stand by the country and by the Constitution. [*cheers*] Let the Union of these States be imprinted in the mind of every man, no matter from what clime he comes from to seek a home in this happy country. [*cheers*] Let us endeavor by all our actions, and by every word we can express, to imprint indelibly upon the minds of young and old that this Constitution must be preserved; and must be handed down to posterity, inviolate. [*enthusiastic applause.*]

The sixth regular toast was then given:

OUR NATIONALITY:

A priceless inheritance, which shall be transmitted inviolate to our children, though with malignant hate and desperate fanaticism, armed traitors at home, envious foes abroad, and reckless incendiaries within our own lines, combine for its destruction.

Hon. CHARLES P. DALY, in responding to the toast, spoke as follows:

FELLOW CITIZENS:

I am called upon to respond to the toast of "Our Nationality." Our nationality is like this bouquet of flowers which the chairman has put into my hand. It is a gathering together of things different in themselves. A mixture of many nationalities bound like this bouquet in confident union. As I hold this up in my hand, it is a beautiful object to look at, but if I cut the string that binds it, it falls to pieces, and the beauty which it had in combination is gone. It has another feature of our nationality. It is largely interspersed with green. [*loud cheering*] Sprigs of green leaves are scattered through it, and gird it around, and support it in an emerald ring. [*cheers*] So that race, the Irish race, of which this color is the emblem and the type, is profusely scattered over the land, a hardy plant, growing up everywhere around the flowers of our common nationality. As this green is to the flowers which keep it company, so in the American Union, the Irish race do not simply adorn, but are one of the the constituent parts of its unity, its strength, and its power.

The GRAND SACHEM gave the seventh regular toast:

ABRAHAM LINCOLN, PRESIDENT OF THE UNITED STATES:

> In so far as he has rejected the trammels of party, overruled the plottings of fanaticism, and been faithful to the Constitution, we honor him. May his future course be such, that the respect and gratitude of his countrymen will be heartfelt and unmixed.

Past Grand Sachem ELIJAH F. PURDY, being called upon to respond, was received with loud cheers for "the old War Horse." He said:

FELLOW DEMOCRATS: One might imagine that it is a mere joke that I am called upon to respond to a toast complimentary to ABRAHAM LINCOLN. Though we live in strange times, I must acknowledge that it is very unusual for me to speak in complimentary terms of any one but a democrat; [*cheers*] but I am really at a loss to find words to express what is really due to the chief magistrate. Whoever may be chief magistrate, he is entitled to the respect and support of every loyal American; and I can assure Mr. LINCOLN, that so long as he conducts this war for the suppression of the rebellion and the supremacy of the law, to restore the Union as it was, and maintaining the Constitution as it is, he will always find a hearty response and cordial support from democrats, [*loud cheers*] and particularly from those of Tammany Hall. [*cheers*] But if this war is to be prosecuted for the dishonest purpose of emancipating the negroes of the South, he cannot expect the support of democrats. [*loud cheers.*] I hope, however, different counsels will prevail; and I believe our present magistrate is disposed and determined to sustain the Constitution as our Fathers made it. [*cheers*] That is all we ask, and as long as he does so—as long as he carries out the principles enunciated by JACKSON, [*cheers*] he may look for the support of all democrats. And I believe, fellow democrats, I but express your feelings when I say that Mr. LINCOLN can do nothing that will gratify us so much as he will by procuring the immediate release of the gallant Colonel CORCORAN. [*enthusiastic cheers.*] In that he may count upon your hearty support. You ask that, and expect it at his hands. [*loud cheers*]

The GRAND SACHEM announced the eighth regular toast:

OUR NOBLE ARMY, AND GEORGE B. McCLELLAN, ITS COMMANDING GENERAL:

The prescient skill and calm self-possession of the young Chief, and the unyielding valor and uncomplaining endurance of all, officers and men, have illuminated with glory the saddest page of our National history.

C. H. BRACKETT, Esq., being loudly called for, arose and responded to the sentiment in a few remarks, in which he depicted in glowing terms the brilliant achievements of our armies, and portrayed with earnest enthusiasm the manly qualities, high abilities and signal services of Gen. McCLELLAN, every mention of whose name elicited prolonged applause.

The ninth regular toast was then given:

OUR GALLANT NAVY:

It has nobly maintained, in the contest with treason, upon our own waters, the unrivalled prestige it acquired in times past by its brilliant victories over a foreign foe, upon the ocean.

Sachem ISAAC BELL, at the call of the GRAND SACHEM, briefly expressed the interest of the metropolis in the triumph and efficiency of the Navy, and the gratification universally diffused by the valiant deeds of FOOTE, DUPONT, FARRAGUT and their gallant associates, his remarks being loudly cheered by a sympathetic audience.

The GRAND SACHEM next gave the tenth regular toast:

THE STATE OF NEW YORK:

Mighty in all the elements of power; in the prompt and generous support which it has given to the War for the Union, it has again vindicated the justice of its motto of "Excelsior."

Responded to by Brother GEORGE W. McLEAN.

The GRAND SACHEM announced the eleventh regular toast:

THE CITY OF NEW YORK:

The Nation has made it great, and overspread the world with
its commerce; and in the struggle for the Nation's life, with
the flowing wealth of its capitalists and the teeming
legions of its soldiers, it has repaid the obligations of duty
and gratitude.

Responded to by Brother ANDRE FROMENT, one of the Alder-
men of the city.

The twelfth regular toast was then given:

THE PRESS:

A mighty engine for good and for evil. Its regulation must
be in and from itself; and it can never be safely subjected
to the arbitrary power of any individual, even though he
be a Cabinet officer.

Responded to by Brother ANSON HERRICK, of the *Atlas*.

The GRAND SACHEM then gave the thirteenth regular toast:

OUR COUNTRYWOMEN:

The inspiration of the soldier's valor and the civilian's labor;
the charm of the household and the blessing of the hos-
pital; upon their hearts war lays its heaviest hand; may
it requite their sacrifices by securing to them and to their
children free and happy homes forever.

Brother HORATIO P. CARR, in a few remarks, gave expression
to the admiration of the Sons of Tammany for the beauties who
grace the Wigwams of the warriors, in a manner which called
forth their rapturous applause.

The proceedings were enlivened by patriotic songs by
FRANCIS B. O'DONNELL and JAMES NESBIT, and the banquet was
concluded with three cheers for Grand Sachem WATERBURY.